# Happy Ever After

ORCHARD BOOKS
338 Euston Road, London NW1 3BH
Orchard Books Australia
Level 17/207 Kent Street, Sydney, NSW 2000

First published in hardback in 2010 by Orchard Books
First published in paperback in 2011

ISBN 978 1 40830 754 0 (HB)
ISBN 978 1 40830 760 1 (PB)

Text © Tony Bradman 2010
Illustrations © Sarah Warburton 2010

A CIP catalogue record for this book is available from the British Library.

1 3 5 7 9 10 8 6 4 2 (HB)
5 7 9 10 8 6 4   (PB)

Printed in Great Britain

Orchard Books is a division of Hachette Children's Books,
an Hachette UK company.
www.hachette.co.uk

# Tony Bradman

# Happy Ever After

# THE WICKED STEPMOTHER
## HELPS OUT

Illustrated by Sarah Warburton

ORCHARD BOOKS

"There you go," said Cinderella, stepping back
to admire her handiwork with a smile.
"A change of hairdo, some funky clothes –
and it's a totally new you!'

The Wicked Stepmother examined herself in the mirror, and she had to agree – Cinderella had done a great job of re-styling her, from top to toe.

Cinderella was married to Prince Charming,
but she had also started her own fashion business
– Cinderella Makeovers Unlimited – and it was
a huge success.

"Thanks, Cinderella," said the Wicked
Stepmother. "You're so good to me, and I really
don't deserve it. I can't believe how horrible
I used to be to you!"

"Oh, stop it!" said Cinderella, giving her a hug.

"All I've done is improve the way you look on the
outside. But you're a different person on the
inside, too. You should be proud of yourself.
Not many people can change like that."

It was true, the Wicked Stepmother had changed rather dramatically. She had felt *so* guilty when the Prince had put the glass slipper on Cinderella's foot and the amazing truth had come out.

That's when she'd realised she had treated poor Cinderella very badly – and she had sworn to be different from then on.

Luckily, Cinderella had completely forgiven her. She had forgiven the Ugly Sisters, too, and these days they both worked for Cinderella. She had given them free makeovers, so they weren't quite as ugly any more. In fact, life for all of them seemed much better…

…although now there was a new problem.

"I'm glad I changed, honestly I am," said the Wicked Stepmother. "But at least being horrible used to keep me busy. Now I'm just so *bored* all the time…"

She let out a deep sigh. Every day was the same. She got up, got dressed and had breakfast, then sat around in her cottage doing…

…well, not very much. She'd certainly had enough of watching daytime programmes on Forest TV.

"I'm sorry to hear that," said Cinderella. "So what would you *like* to do?"

"I'd like to help people," said the Wicked Stepmother. "That way I could make up for all the bad stuff I did. I don't know how to go about it, though."

"What a wonderful idea!" said Cinderella.
"It sounds to me as if you need some advice –
and I happen to know exactly the right person
to give it to you."

Cinderella made a quick phone call, then
gave the Wicked Stepmother an address.
It was the palace where Princess Daisy lived
with her husband Prince Freddy. He was famous
for having been turned into a frog by a witch.
But now he was human again, and he and
his wife ran all the charities in the Forest.

"As you can see, helping people is definitely what we're all about here," said Princess Daisy. She gave the Wicked Stepmother a whirlwind tour of their large office, which seemed very busy.

"There's a huge range of things you could get involved in. Although maybe you should start with something simple…"

"And what could be simpler than going collecting for us?" said Prince Freddy with a big grin. "We often need money to help people."

Later that morning, the Wicked Stepmother found herself standing at the crossroads in the Forest. She was wearing a bright orange jacket with the name of the charity she was collecting for – *The Ugly Duckling Trust* – written across the back of it. She also had a collecting tin.

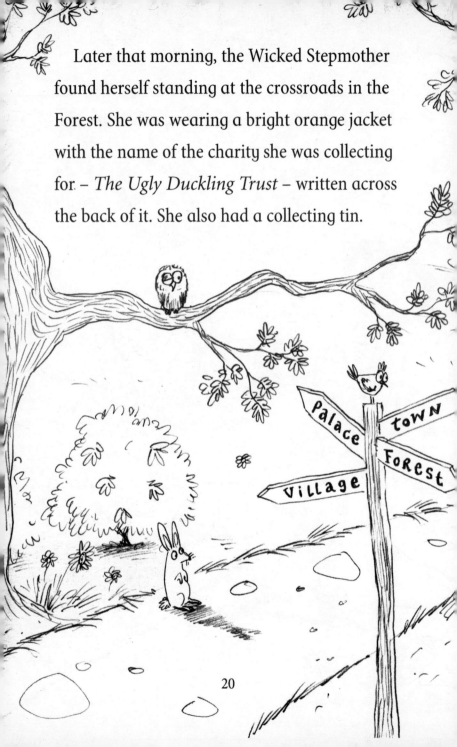

It was a cold day, and there weren't many
people about. A couple of young trolls ran by
and stuck their tongues out at her.

Mr Wolf trotted past and said he was sorry,
but he didn't have any money to spare.

And then a nasty old king rode up and ordered her to get out of his way – she was blocking the road!

· The Wicked Stepmother very nearly lost her temper – and then it started to rain.

She trudged back through the Forest to report
back to Daisy and Freddy.

"Let's see, that's, er…one fake farthing, three
buttons, and an acorn," said Daisy. "Oh dear,
that didn't go too well. How about trying
something else?"

"C-c-could it be indoors?" murmured the
Wicked Stepmother, shivering.

"I've got just the thing," said Prince Freddy
with a smile. "Come with me."

He took her to a small, dusty room with
a single desk in it. On the desk stood a great
tottering tower of unopened letters, and
a phone that was ringing.

Prince Freddy explained that the letters had
been sent by people asking for help, and that he
and Daisy needed someone to read them all.

"I think I can manage that," said the Wicked
Stepmother, and sat down.

"Er, it would be great if you could answer the
phone too," said Freddy.

The next couple of hours were tough for the Wicked Stepmother. She started reading the letters, and soon she was engrossed in the sad stories they contained.

Then the phone started ringing…

…but the stories she heard were even sadder than those in the letters.

By the time she spoke to an old woman
who lived in a shoe, who had so many children
she just didn't know what to do, the
Wicked Stepmother was in tears.

"Ah, this doesn't seem to be going well either,"
said Daisy, handing the Wicked Stepmother
a tissue. "Not to worry, there must be
*something* for you."

But there wasn't. That night the Wicked
Stepmother went home to her empty little cottage.
If she couldn't work for a charity, what could
she do? She was beginning to think she would
never help anyone…

The next morning the Wicked Stepmother went to see Cinderella for a chat. But just as she was going into Cinderella's boutique, she bumped into someone she recognised.

"Oh hi, it's the Terrible Ogre, isn't it?" she said. "What are you doing here?"

"I've come for a makeover," said the Terrible Ogre miserably. "Although to be honest, it's not what I look like that needs an overhaul, it's my personality."

"Really? *Tell* me about it," said the Wicked Stepmother, and smiled. But she was interested too. "There was a time not that long ago when I felt the same…"

So the Wicked Stepmother and the
Terrible Ogre sat and talked over a nice
cup of camomile tea.

It turned out the Terrible Ogre was fed up with himself. He had made a lot of people unhappy, and wanted to change. But he didn't know how.

The Wicked Stepmother listened, and made
some suggestions.

"Thank you *so* much!" the Terrible Ogre said quietly at last. "You're the first person I've met who's made me feel that I really *can* change if I want to."

"No problem," said the Wicked Stepmother. "I was only trying to help."

"You've helped me a lot," said the Terrible Ogre. "Hey, I bet you could help others like me, too. You ought to do this kind of thing for a living. Cheerio!"

"Oh right, bye!" said the Wicked Stepmother.
"Umm, helping others like him…" she murmured.
And then she grinned. "What a truly
*excellent* idea!"

The one thing she knew about was how to change from being bad to being good. And there were plenty of characters in the Forest who needed to do just that. She talked it over with Cinderella, who gave her some terrific advice about setting up a business.

A couple of weeks later, the Wicked Stepmother opened the Fairy Tale Clinic for Recovering Villains. Her first client was the Terrible Ogre, but she soon had many more.

She treated witches and giants and even some
other stepmothers. She spent every day helping
people, and they were all very grateful.

The Wicked Stepmother was just happy
to be busy…

…but in a good way.

FINDING
the
NICE PERSON
WITHIN YOU

12 Steps

1 ___
2 ___

And so, strangely enough, the Wicked Stepmother and every villain in the Forest who walked through the doors of her clinic managed to live…

*…HAPPILY EVER AFTER!*